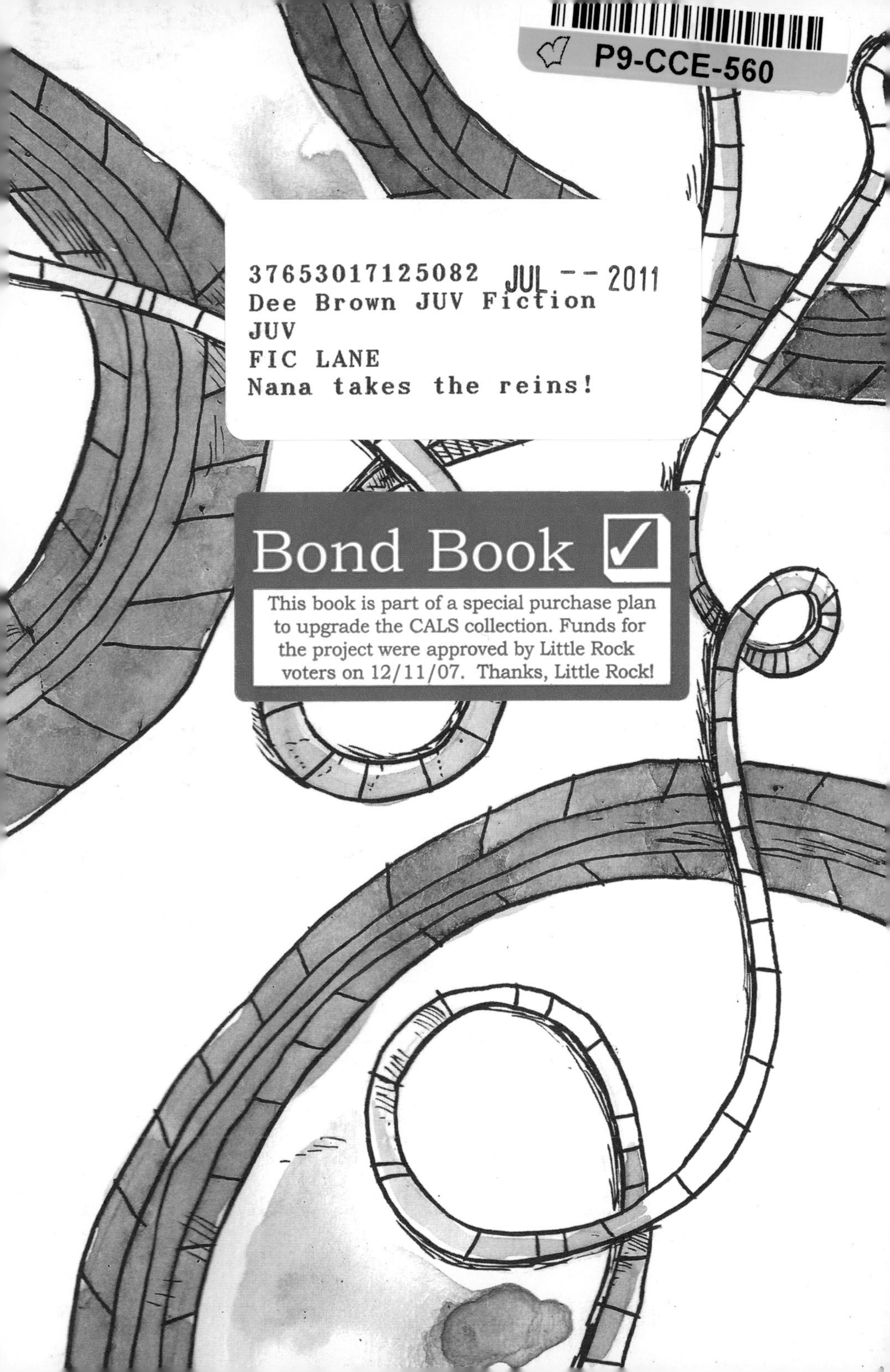

Nana TAKES THE REINS!

By Kathleen Lane, with Cabell Harris
Illustrated by Sarah Horne

chronicle books · san francisco

For Leo and John Kentucky.
— K. L. —

To my Nana, Selma Letitia Schumann, and my children's Nana, Shirley Schumann Harris. Between them they have provided a lifetime supply of stories.
— C. H. —

For my Auntie Liz, with love.
— S. H. —

Library of Congress Cataloging-in-Publication Data available.
ISBN 978-0-8118-6260-8

Book design by Eloise Leigh.
Typeset in Plantin.
The illustrations in this book were rendered in in.

Manufactured by C & C Offset, Langgang, Shenzhen, China, in November 2010.

10 9 8 7 6 5 4 3 2 1

This product conforms to CPSIA 2008.

Chronicle Books LLC
680 Second Street, San Francisco, California 94107

www.chroniclekids.com

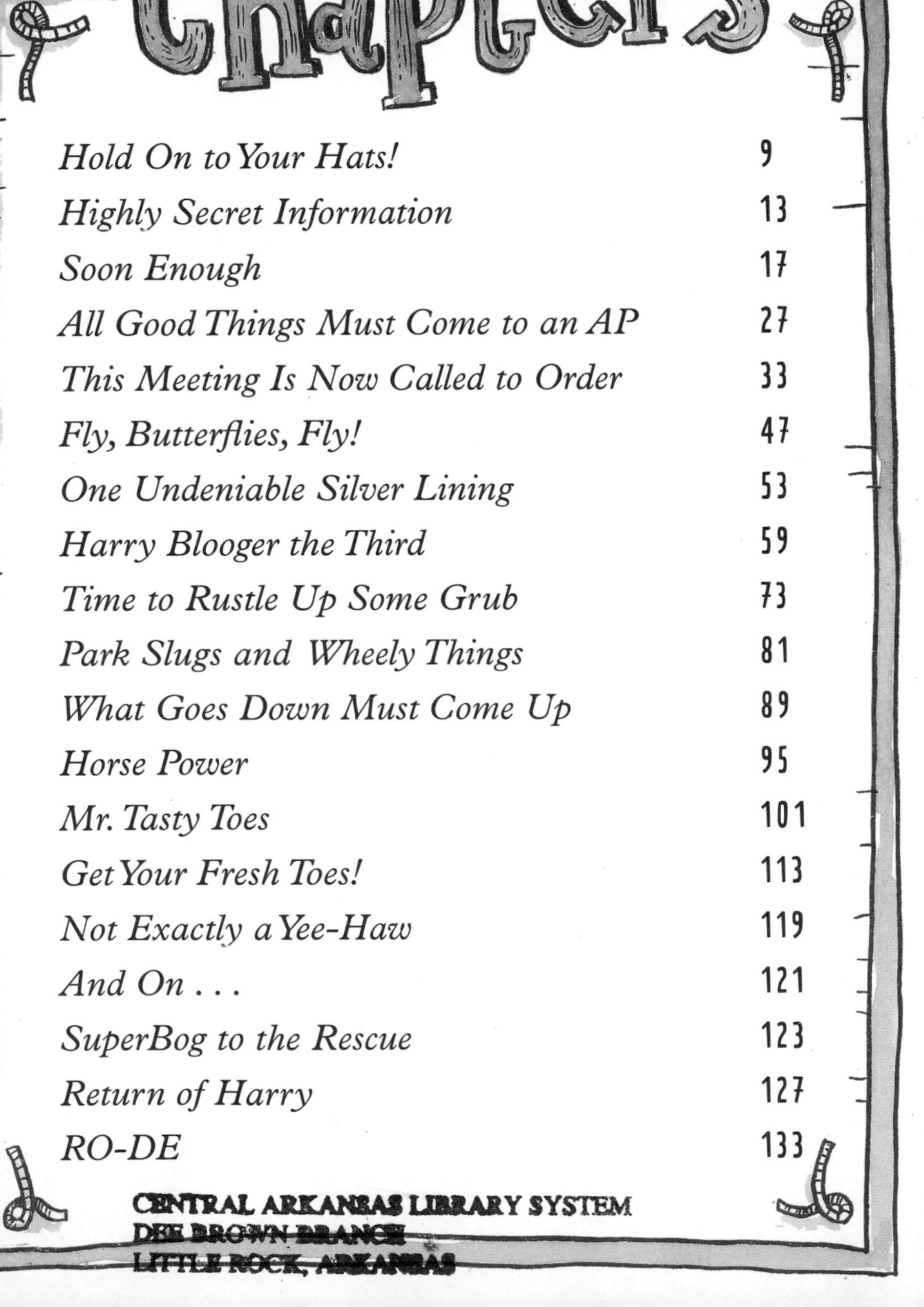

Chapters

BULL RIDERS
BULL RIDERS
GRAB YOUR SADDLES AND
HEAD TO THE FAIRGROUNDS.
THE LETTUCEBERG
COUNTY RODEO IS
HERE!
MECHANIC NEEDED
EXPERT IN RATTLES, SHIMMERS,
CLANGS, KABONGS, PEETERS, PUTTERS
AND ZBONGS, APPLY AT AL'S BRAKE SHOP

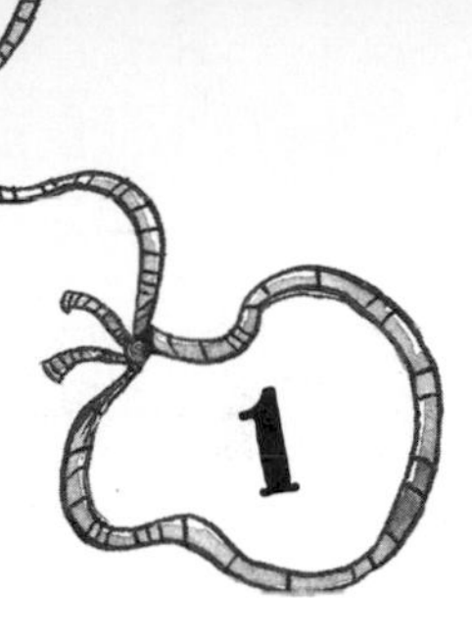

Hold On to Your Hats!

"Bull riding!" exclaimed Nana. "What fun! I haven't ridden a bull in years." Nana felt around the table for her scissors and accidentally picked up a Fudge Freezie wrapper instead.

"Or was it a mule?" she said, putting down the Fudge Freezie wrapper and picking up another one. "Yes, I believe it was a mule. Well . . . mule . . . bull . . . they can't be all that different."

"Oh dear, where did my scissors run off to?"

Nana picked up her box of Sugar Puffies—no scissors—and her tin of strawberry swirl meringues—no scissors—and her choco-coated-coconut-crunchies—no scissors.

"Aha! There you are!" she said when she spotted the sneaky snippers peeking out from under a book.

Nana quickly cut the rodeo advertisement out of the paper, tucked it inside her purse, and headed out the door.

Her 1948 Dusty Drifter sat in the driveway, and though her daughter, Elaine, insisted she give up driving on the grounds that she was much too old, Nana could not see the harm

in one little trip to the fairgrounds. Besides, unbeknownst to Elaine, Nana was quite a skilled (if creative) driver.

"Now then," said Nana. She climbed into the Dusty Drifter and gave the old car a pat on the dashboard. "To the rodeo we go." And with a sharp turn this way, a curly turn that way, and a *beep beep* for good measure (Nana did so love to toot her horn), she was on her way.

NO POINT IN GOING AROUND.
WEEEE!
HERE SQUIRRELY SQUIRRELY SQUIRRELY
BAKERY
ONE SPRINKLE CRINKLE PLEASE!

Highly Secret Information

As she hopped across the Barley Bridge (which was much more fun than simply driving), Nana thought about what a marvelous coincidence it was that here she was about to become a bull rider when only moments ago she had been reading about rodeos in *The Egg Pickler's Companion*.

Oh dear, perhaps that sounds a bit odd. Especially if you are not familiar with Nana's library. (If you *are* familiar with Nana's library, you may skip along to chapter 3 or spend the next several paragraphs humming yourself a lovely tune.)

As for the rest of you, now let's see. How best to explain Nana's library? Well, as you may have learned from your mother, or perhaps a teacher once said something about it, one must never judge a book by its cover. That is especially, particularly, and most exceedingly the case when the book and the cover happen to reside in the home of Nana. In Nana's house, you see, books and covers are entirely different matters altogether.

You might, for example, find a book called *The Joy of Napping* on one of Nana's shelves, but if you were to have a look inside, you would not feel the least bit sleepy. For within its covers you would discover a colorful history of the circus, complete with foldout posters and tips on lion feeding, tightrope prancing, and other such maneuvers.

Likewise, if you flipped through the pages of *The Egg Pickler's Companion*, you would not find a single boiled egg, but instead a detailed diagram of the correct arm movements for roping a cactus from twenty yards away.

Peculiar, yes. But to anyone acquainted with Nana's daughter, Elaine, this cover swapping business is a very logical—and in fact necessary—thing to do.

Elaine, you see, is the very worst kind of cheek-biting worrier. If she were to discover that Nana was studying up on the profession of bull riding, there would be disastrous consequences indeed. Not only would she take to twisting her arm hairs right out of their follicles, but there is a very good chance she would have Nana moved to that place for old people, that very dreary place where Elaine worked and where she was convinced that Nana belonged.

So now, along with Eufala and Bog, you are an official keeper of the secret. But, oh dear, if you are not familiar with Nana's library then that means you have not yet met Nana's grandchildren.

Well, no matter. You will meet them soon enough.

THE JOY OF NAPPIN

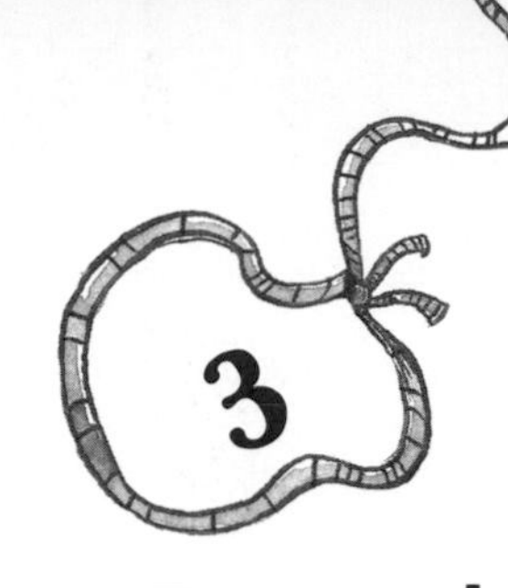

Soon Enough

There's nothing like a summer morning. The cool morning air. The *chiffity chiff chiff* of sprinklers. The big family trip to the grocery store to buy sour cream.

No? This is not how you spend your summer mornings? Well, consider yourself lucky. Poor Eufala and Bog are not so fortunate. In fact, while most children in the neighborhood were pumping up their beach balls, Eufala and Bog were putting on their coats and strapping on their sandals because just moments ago their mother said, "Put on your coats and sandals. We're going to the store to buy sour cream."

"Can't we go swimming instead?" asked Eufala.

It was a useless plea, almost as useless as Bog's "I know! Maybe we can drive to the beach."

"Well," said their mother, "we are out of sour cream, and if we don't go get sour cream then . . . well . . . well then . . . "

"We won't have sour cream?" suggested Bog.

"Yes," said their mother. "And then what would we do?"

"Not have any sour cream?" said Eufala.

"Exactly," said their mother. "And is that what you want?"

Before Eufala could say "Yes"—because nothing would have made her happier than just one meal without sour cream—their mother said, "Come along now, children. We don't have all day." (Actually, without any plans at all—no picnics or parks or Popsicle stands—they did, in fact, have all day.)

Elaine led the way down Vinegar Street, her grocery list pinched between her fingers. True, there was only one item on the list, but Elaine enjoyed lists so very much that she wrote one out nonetheless. "Sour cream," it said in tiny block letters perfectly centered within the margins of her notepad.

Their walk to the grocery store was all *watch out fors* and *keep away froms*. With her chin raised high and her nostrils flared wide, Elaine called back over her shoulder:

"Watch out for that dog."

"Keep away from that spill."

"Watch out for that unicycle."

"Keep away from that monkey." (And, fair enough, you never can tell what a monkey will do.)

"Watch out for that stinkbug."

"Keep away from that sneezeweed."

"Watch out for that . . . that *thing*."

Eufala and Bog followed along behind their mother, being sure to run their fingers along every leaf and dip their shoes into every sticky spill they passed as their mother continued to call back:

"Watch out for that squirrel."

"Keep away from that nail." (Which Eufala pocketed, naturally.)

"Watch out for that bun." (*A perfectly good raisin bun*, thought Bog, *if you scrape off the dirt*.)

"Keep away from that—"

And then, she stopped.

It was a very good thing Elaine's eyesight was not so good, for what caught her not-so-good eyes just then, what made her stop cold in the middle of the sidewalk, was a car hopping (yes, hopping) by in the opposite direction. A car that looked very much like Nana's car, with a driver that looked very much like Nana's hair.

"Is that Nana?"

Eufala and Bog had stopped, too, and were holding their breath and saying silent prayers

that their mother's eyes had somehow grown even worse in the last seven seconds.

"Nana?" said Bog.

"Nana who?" said Eufala. She then tried distracting her mother by pointing into the air and shouting, "Monarch!" It was the only butterfly she could ever remember, but the tactic was worth a try, for she knew her mother could never resist a butterfly.

When a Monarch failed to miraculously appear before them, Eufala had to think quickly. "Oh Mother, please can I have it?" she squealed, jumping up and down and pointing at the display window behind them. "Please, please, please, I just love it. Can I have it?"

Eufala, of course, had only meant to pull her mother's attention away from Nana and had not considered the fact that what she was pointing at was a vacuum cleaner attachment.

Why would a person want a vacuum cleaner attachment? Yes, this question occurred to Eufala as well. And what's worse, she could not think of one single reason that she should suddenly need to have one.

She searched the window for something else. Then, though she did not feel very confident about her next selection either, she carefully adjusted the angle of her arm to point at a mop, and declared, so loudly that Bog nearly bit off the finger he had been nibbling on since the whole catastrophe began, "I want to be a witch for Halloween!"

True, it was only June, but it was never too early to begin thinking about one's costume.

Elaine turned briefly to look in the window, but it did not seem that she had been listening to Eufala at all. Almost instantly, her gaze shifted back to that car, which fortunately was quite far away now, and also a bit hazy, what with all the smoke. (We'll get to that shortly.)

Meanwhile, Bog, with two years less experience in tactics of distraction and trickery, began jumping up and down on both feet crying, "I broke my leg! I broke my leg!" This, of course, was not only completely implausible but made the whole effort appear much more suspicious.

And so, as a way of bumping up the quality of Bog's inferior lie, Eufala promptly kicked him in the shin, causing him to holler "Ow! Ow, ow, ow, ow!" so convincingly that their mother immediately dropped to her knees to examine the break.

"Are you sure that wasn't Nana?" asked Elaine, after she had deemed Bog's leg miraculously healed. (In fact, as you will soon see, it was in perfect working order.)

By this time, with Nana's car safely around the corner, Eufala and Bog could use all of their acting skills, as well as a few of their gymnastics skills, to appear as if they were searching high and low for Nana.

"Where?" asked Bog, rocking left to right.

"Where?" asked Eufala, stretching up and down.

Which was exactly the opening Bog had been waiting for.

"Ow!" hollered Eufala. "Ow, ow, ow, ow!"

All Good Things Must Come to an AP

As for Nana, let's just say that not all things in life go according to plan. This is particularly true when one is driving a 1948 Dusty Drifter.

With a rusty muffler.

And a broken taillight.

And three flat tires.

And one very tall steering wheel.

Everything went fine along Paprika Street. Vinegar Street was a breeze as well—though a somewhat smoky breeze. But then, turning onto Churning Avenue (by way of the duck pond), the trouble began. Maybe it was the quadruple mailbox loop-de-loop. Or perhaps it was the high-speed pond glide with a reverse half twist. At any rate, it started with a sputter, which soon turned into a cough, followed by several quacks. Actually, scratch the quacks; they came from the duck.

Next came a snort, followed by what sounded like the opening notes of the "Star Spangled Banner" as sung by a bullfrog.

And lastly:

BRAAAAAP.............

AP.....

AAP!

AP...

"Oh my," said Nana, climbing out of her car to have a look. "That didn't sound so good, did it?"

No, it certainly didn't. And, in fact, Nana's chances of becoming a bull rider suddenly looked about as slim as a one-legged walking stick.

But we must look on the bright side, thought Nana, who was quite skilled at finding silver linings, as difficult to locate as they could sometimes be.

It helps, of course, if you hum a tune.

And so, as Nana walked around and around the Dusty Drifter, looking for just where to begin, she hummed herself a happy tune.

"Well," she said when she spotted the duck on top of her car, "I suppose I shall begin with you." She lifted the duck from the roof and began smoothing its feathers, which were quite fluffed from the journey.

"I do believe," said Nana, "that I owe you an apology."

QUICK!
QUICK!

“Quick,” said the duck. He had meant to say “quack,” but his quacker was a bit out of whack (as you can imagine, after such an ordeal).

Nevertheless, Nana did her best to accommodate. Quick as she could, she apologized to the duck for the great inconvenience of removing him from his home on the pond.

She then resumed her walk around the car, this time with her feathered companion waddling along behind. “Now let’s see,” she said, “where might that silver lining be?”

5 This Meeting Is Now Called to Order

While normally Eufala and Bog dragged their feet behind their mother, now it was Elaine who did the lollygagging. And it was Eufala and Bog this time, not their mother, who walked with long strides and upturned chins.

"Hurry, Mother," urged Eufala.

"We have to get home," insisted Bog, for they were both quite anxious to discuss what Nana was up to—and even more importantly, how they could get in on what Nana was up to.

All three of them were so twisted up in thought that instead of continuing on their way to the grocery store, they had turned around and started back home. Elaine had even managed to forget all about the sour cream. In fact, only three words ran through her mind: *what*, *on*, and *earth*.

"What on earth?" she mumbled as she dragged her feet behind the children. Though she had little proof, Elaine often got the strangest feeling that Nana was up to something. She just never knew exactly what the something was. For every time she found a clue as to what the something might be, such as a muddy pair of work boots next to Nana's house shoes, the clue would disappear and be replaced by a completely different clue, such as an acrobat's baton poking out from the umbrella stand.

But then all Elaine had to do was remind herself that Nana was entirely too old to do anything but . . . well . . . be very old.

And so it was again. By the time they reached home, Elaine found herself shaking her head and laughing at herself for even thinking that it could have been Nana's 1948 Dusty Drifter. "Of course not. How silly of me," she muttered as she led the children into the house, which always carried the faint smell of sauerkraut and bleach.

After removing their coats and shoes, Eufala and Bog tore off their clothes and made for the tub. Oh yes, this is new information, isn't it? The children's baths.

As you know, Elaine is a bit of a worrier. And one of the things that worriers love most to worry about is (and here they will often shudder at the very thought) the bacterial germ. And so, unlike most children who take one bath a day *at most*, Eufala and Bog were required to take three: a morning bath, an after-lunch bath, and one more in the evening before bed. They were, despite their best efforts to the contrary, perhaps the squeakiest children in all of Lettuceberg.

Eufala washed behind her ears in record time. Bog nearly took the skin off his shins, so rigorous was his scrubbing. And then it was a flickery of towels as the children dried themselves off and got into new clothes—oh heavens no, not the same clothes they had just worn that morning.

Finally, the children arranged themselves, knees to knees, on Eufala's bed for a meeting of utmost importance.

First order of business: candy.

Bog, chair of the candy committee, divided the gummy rats he had pulled from their secret hiding place—which, for security purposes,

cannot be mentioned here—and the children each tucked a handful of chewies into their cheeks. It's not that they weren't eager to get on to more important matters. It's just that over the years they had found (and perhaps you have, too) that it is much easier to think when one has sweets tucked in one's cheeks.

"Okay," said Eufala, after she had arranged the rats in a neat row along the outside of her bottom teeth, "We have to figure out where Nana was going. She had to be going *somewhere*."

"Maybe she was going to the circus," said Bog, growing more excited with each word. "Yeah," he said, "and she was on her way to pick us up and . . . "

"Bog," said Eufala, "the circus left town last week. Remember?"

"Oh yeah," said Bog, who had especially hoped to see the lion tamer put his head inside the lion's mouth. "Then maybe she's taking us to Happy Land?"

"Bog!" A gummy rat popped out of Eufala's mouth and landed on her knee. "Happy Land's like a thousand miles away."

"It was just an idea."

Eufala returned the rat to its place in line and said, "Look. Forget what Nana's doing. The question is, how are we going to get out of here?" It wasn't the first time the children had asked themselves this very question.

"Yeah," said Bog. "What are we going to do?"

"I don't know."

Eufala thought of all of the ideas they had tried before. They couldn't say they were going back to school for extra homework, not in June. They couldn't say they wanted to take some cookies to old Mrs. McCrotchity across the street, because Mrs. McCrotchity asked their mother to please not send them over anymore. Maybe it was because last time they nearly gave her a heart attack when they practically threw the cookies at her and screamed,

"Hi, Mrs. McCrotchity! Bye, Mrs. McCrotchity!" before running off to do whatever it was they had escaped to do.

"I don't know either," said Bog, who had been over and over his list of ideas, too.

"Well, we have to think of something," said Eufala.

"Yeah," said Bog. "What should we do?"

"I don't know," said Eufala.

"Me neither," said Bog. "Do you have any ideas?"

"No, I just told you that."

"Oh yeah."

"Shhhh. I'm trying to think."

"Did you think of anything yet?"

"Bog, you have to be quiet so I can think."

"Oh yeah."

And so on . . . and so on . . . until finally Eufala screamed, "Sour cream!"

Never had those two words sounded so beautiful to her ears. "We forgot to get the sour cream!"

Of course! Why didn't they think of it before?

"Actually," said Bog, "I was just about to say that."

"No, you weren't," said Eufala, and quickly placed a finger in each ear so she wouldn't have to listen to her brother's babbling as she led the way down the hall.

As expected, they found their mother sitting at the dining room table with her butterfly specimens laid out in neat rows. She held a magnifying glass in one hand and a *Bog Fritillary* in the other. Elaine often passed long hours at the table examining her butterflies, a fact the children counted on whenever they needed to attend to their more mischievous affairs.

"Mother," said Eufala, in her most darling voice (imagine a tiny fairy singing atop a pile of pink petals). "Would you like us to go . . . "

"Get sour cream for you?" interrupted Bog, smiling like a cherub despite the hole his sister's glare was burning into the side of his face.

"Oh!" gasped their mother. "The sour cream! I forgot the sour cream!"

"Yes, Mother," said Eufala. "And if we don't go get sour cream then . . . "

"We won't have any sour cream," said Bog.

"And then what would we do?" added Eufala.

"You're absolutely right." Elaine began to set the *Bog Fritillary* back into its tray, though it looked as if her fingers were having difficulty letting go. "I'll just get my purse," she said, looking down at the furry gray-brown moth as if it were the most beautiful creature she had ever laid eyes on.

"That's okay," said Eufala, who saw her only hope shrinking before her eyes. "I mean, I think we're responsible enough to walk to the store on our own."

Responsible in all its forms and synonyms was a word that Elaine liked very much. It was as sweet to her ears as *lepidoptera*.

Elaine looked at her children, who looked as if they could use another bath, then at the butterfly pinched between her tweezers.

"My purse is in the kitchen," she said. "Watch for cars, don't talk to strangers, and . . . and put your coats on."

"But it's ninety-three degrees—" Bog started.

"Yes, Mother!" Eufala interrupted, yanking her brother out of the room.

"And your hats!" called their mother. "And keep away from . . . " But soon her words turned fuzzy, her worries grew wings, and, lowering her tweezers, she gently set her *Bog Fritillary* back down into its tray and ever so lovingly lifted out another of her favorite specimens, the *Lerodea Eufala*.

Eufala and Bog did as they were told. First and most important stop: their mother's purse.

Eufala pulled out two twenty-dollar bills, and Bog went in for a third. How were they to know, after all, how much sour cream costs?

They then pulled on their hats and coats and headed out the door, where they immediately pulled off their hats and coats and dropped them behind the rhododendron bush.

"She never said to *keep* them on," said Eufala.

"I didn't hear her say to keep them on," agreed Bog, flapping his arms in the warm morning air.

And away, as the saying goes, they flew.

Z
Z
Z
THE JOY OF NAPPING

Fly, Butterflies, Fly!

Eufala and Bog took every shortcut known to Lettuceberg, along with a few of their very own, such as the one through Mrs. Myrtlewood's living room. (Mrs. Myrtlewood, a devoted follower of Dr. Hordemeyer's *Joy of Napping* book, could often be found dozing on her divan.)

Arriving back at the spot where they had last seen Nana's car, Eufala and Bog found only an empty street.

Well, almost empty.

Except for the muffler.

And the rearview mirror.

"And this," said Bog, picking up a tailpipe.

"And that," said Eufala, running past her brother to a headlight.

There is no need to tell you where this trail of parts eventually led. Since your mind is no doubt well ahead of Eufala and Bog's legs, let's just speed on down the road and around the corner to where, you guessed it, one very wet . . . and muddy . . . and grassy . . . and ducky Dusty Drifter smoked and heaved on the side of the road. There beside it, unwinding a kite string from around the Drifter's antenna, stood Nana, quite unharmed and as cheerful as ever.

"Oh good!" she said when she spotted her grandchildren. "Just the two to accompany me to the rodeo." (Little did Eufala and Bog know, of course, that Nana planned to be *in* the rodeo.)

Naturally, Eufala and Bog were overjoyed at the thought. A real rodeo. They had never in their lives been to a real rodeo. They had never even been to a real ranch. The closest they ever came to experiencing a ranch was in its salad dressing form, which they were permitted only on special occasions.

"RO-DE-O!" they chanted, "RO-DE-O! RO-DE-O!" oh, about fifty-seven times, though the last several rounds sounded considerably less enthusiastic. For right around number fifty-three, it began to occur to them that in their arms they held a good portion of the car that would be taking them to the rodeo.

"Ro . . . de . . . " Bog looked down at the rusted tailpipe he had tucked up under his arm. "O."

"Um, Nana?" said Eufala, a hubcap slipping from her arms and clattering to the ground. "How are we going to get to the rodeo?"

They all looked at the car. Smoke curled from the hood; water dripped from the trunk. It looked pretty hopeless alright. Less than hopeless. It looked hopelessless . . . especially to two children who had not yet learned the virtues of positive thinking. In fact, as far as Eufala and Bog were concerned, there was only one appropriate response to such a situation:

Pouting.

Eufala dropped down onto the curb and began tossing pebbles at a hubcap. Bog consoled himself with a licorice rope.

The duck consoled himself from the other end.

Which is too bad, really. For if they had not been so busy contorting their faces into various expressions of disappointment and agony, they might have been the ones to discover it. After all, it was not more than ten feet away from them.

AL'S
BRAKE shop

7

One Undeniable Silver Lining

If Eufala and Bog had only turned around, they would have seen that little sign nailed to the wooden post. But as Nana was the only one whose chin was angled up, the honor fell to her.

"Ah, there we go," she said, not in the least surprised by this sudden good fortune. "A mechanic's shop."

Eufala and Bog leaped to their feet, spun around, and stared at the little hand-lettered sign.

"Look!" shouted Eufala, racing up to another sign a little farther up Butter Street.

"Now let's see," said Nana. "How about I go

see about our car while you two run off and get us some snacks for the rodeo?"

So Eufala and Bog ran off to the Buy-n-Buy, and Nana headed to Al's Brake Shop, which, according to the signs, was located down at the end of Butter Street.

Actually, that's not quite true.

Al's Brake Shop, as you can see, was located *up* at the end of Butter Street.

In fact, the precise location of Al's Brake Shop was *up up up* at the end of Butter Street. Have a look for yourself:

Not the most fortunate location for a mechanic's shop, if you think about it. Go ahead and think about it. We'll wait.

That's right. Broken down cars are not so good at motoring up to the tops of hills, are they? But poor Al didn't think of this rather important detail when he first saw that empty building there on the top of Butter Street. In fact, on that crisp October morning with the air smelling so sweetly of battery fluid, Al did not even see that hill. (What hill?) And if there had been a six-headed dragon up there, too, well, he wouldn't have paid it the least attention.

The hill certainly did not go unnoticed by Nana, however, who was all huffs and puffs when she finally arrived up top and inside the door to Al's Brake Shop.

“He . . . he . . . he” she said to Al, who was standing behind the counter. “He . . . he . . . he . . . ” and finally “. . . llo.”

Nana then proceeded to tell Al about her car, which, as winded as she was, took quite some time. In fact, for your reading ease, all puffing and panting has been removed from the following sentence:

“I’m afraid it’s lost its oomph,” said Nana. “And it’s very important that I get it repaired, you see, as I am on my way to the rodeo to become a bull rider.”

Al began to open his mouth (actually it was already opened quite wide at Nana’s mention of bull riding), but before he could manage to speak, the door swung open, with such force that it blew Nana’s hair up into a cotton candy swirl.

There in the doorway stood a very large man with a very small head.

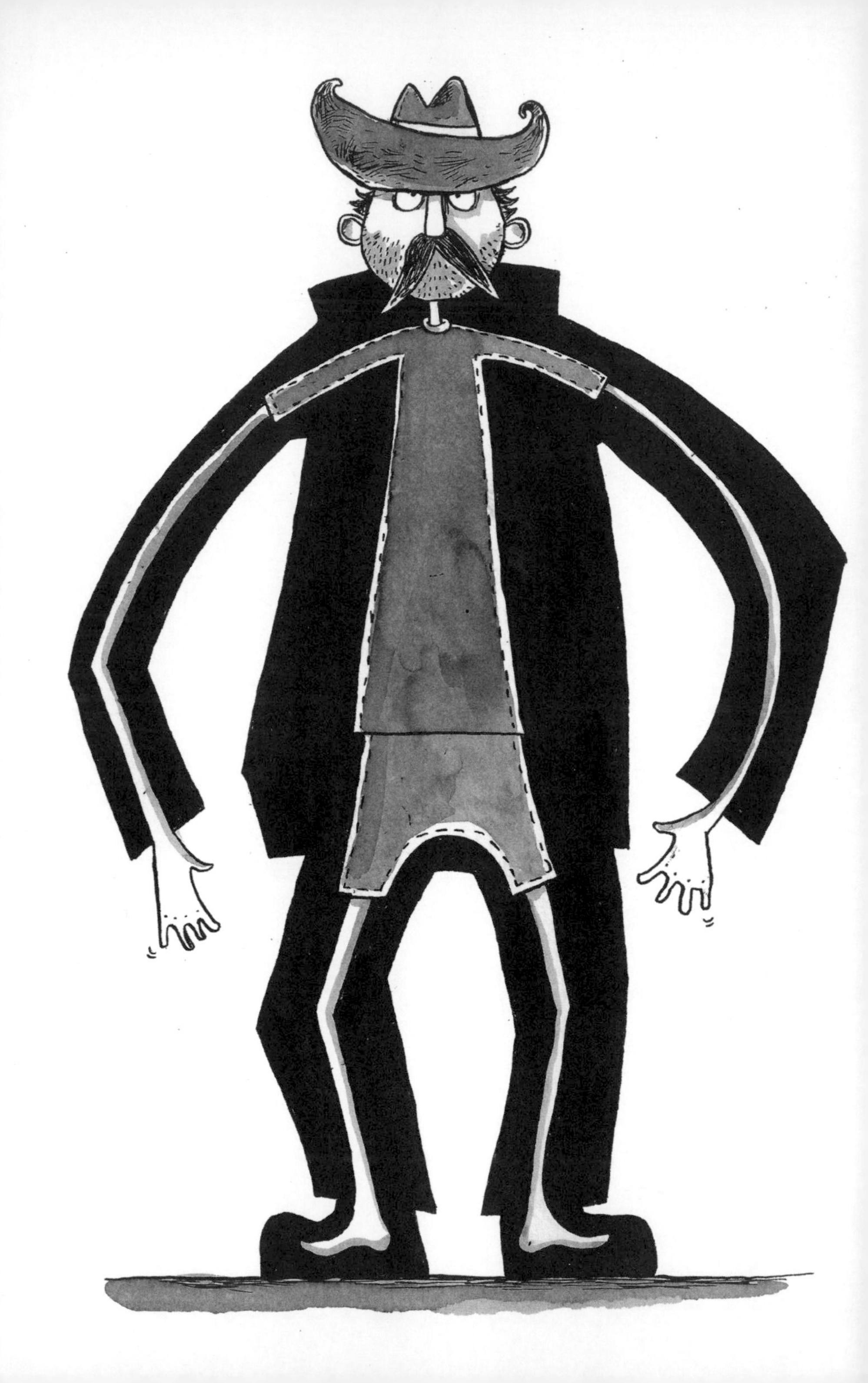

Harry Blooger the Third

Though Nana did not yet know this, the man's name was Tuff. And there was something else she did not know. In fact, nobody in all of Crispy County, not even the seven men standing behind Tuff (we'll get to them shortly), knew this secret: In truth, Tuff was not a very large man at all. If you took away his leather coat and the leather vest underneath it, and the leather undershirt underneath the leather vest, and the leather chaps and the leather pants and the leather boxers underneath the leather pants, he was . . . well, he looked a bit like a cornstalk. In fact, considering his broomlike physique,

Tuff's head was pretty much the size it ought to be.

And oh, Tuff's real name? Harry Blooger the Third.

(But it's best if you don't call him that.)

Now Tuff and his gang of Ruffies were not, shall we say, the most appreciated citizens of Lettuceberg.

For one thing, they ate house pets.

Or that was the rumor anyway. No one had actually ever seen a Ruffy eating a hamster, or even a gecko, but anyone in Lettuceberg would tell you that this was, in fact, a bona fide, grade-A, honest-to-goodness fact.

AND NOT ONLY THAT, THEY PULL WINGS OFF BIRDS.
AND BLOW THIER NOSES INTO HAMBURGER BUNS.
AND NOT ONLY THAT, THEY STEAL PEOPLE'S SHOES, SOMETIMES WITH THEIR FEET STILL IN THEM.
THEN THEY EAT THEIR TOES.
FIRST THEY ROAST THEM ON STICKS.
THEN THEY EAT THEM. WHICH IS WHY THEIR TEETH ARE BLACK. FROM EATING SO MANY TOES WITHOUT BRUSHING THEIR TEETH.

At least, those were the rumors.

But rumors, as you might imagine, had a way of skipping over Nana. They would simply fly past her ears and into the ears of the next person. And that is why when Tuff stomped up to the counter, Nana did not see any reason that she shouldn't stomp right up next to him. She wanted to hear what the gentleman had to say.

"Got a spark plug out," he said, in a voice so loud that it made Nana teeter a bit to one side. "I'll be back at noon to pick her up."

The man reminded Nana a bit of her Uncle Wendell, who used to entertain the children by crushing lightbulbs inside his armpits. Oh, what good times they used to have.

Unfortunately, Tuff did not bring up such pleasant memories for poor Al. Far far from it. You see, Al and Tuff had known each other a good many years—or you might say, a *bad* many years—and over the course of those bad many years, poor Al had consumed enough antacids to fill up the Crispy County public pool. On the bright side, though, he still had all of his toes—fingers, too, thank goodness. And though he kept his pet bunny, Bumper, under the counter behind a bundle of rags, not once did he arrive at work to find him missing, or even chewed upon.

"Uh gee, Harry . . . I–I mean Tuff" said Al, "I wish I could help you, but . . ."

"Uh gee, Tuff," repeated Tuff in a high-pitched voice. Then, dropping down into a K9

growl, he added, "Get it done by noon, or I'll flatten you into a floor mat."

Oh my, thought Nana, *someone could use a little lesson in manners*.

"Well see, the only problem is—," said Al.

"And wipe my feet on you," said Tuff.

"Okay, Tuff, but the thing is, see, I'm a little short on mechanics—"

"You wouldn't want us to take our business down to Buddy's, would you?"

You would think that this would be exactly what Al would want, but because of the already mentioned unfortunate location of his shop (and the fortunate location of Buddy's Garage down the hill), poor Al was lucky to have any business at all. The Ruffies not only didn't mind hoisting their cars up to the top of the hill, but for some unknown reason, they appeared to actually *enjoy* it.

Without the Ruffies, difficult as they may be, Al might as well board the place up. And so what

could he say to Tuff but, "Gosh, Tuff, I wouldn't want you to do that."

Tuff let out one last growl and stomped out of the shop, leaving behind a chorus of rattling wrenches and clanging cup holders. He and the other Ruffies then climbed into their cars, fired up their engines, and rumbled off down the hill.

Al wiped his forehead with a rag, leaving an oily smudge in the precise shape of a baby's bonnet. "What a fix," he moaned. "What a fix."

He had only three mechanics, and all three of them were already working on other Ruffy cars, each dropped off with a worse threat than the one before. One Ruffy said he'd crush Al into a cup holder if he didn't get his car done by lunch. Another said he'd stuff him up a muffler. And the third told Al that if he didn't fix his car by sundown, he'd turn him into furry dice and hang him from his rearview mirror.

Al tucked his rag back into the pocket of his overalls and reached beneath the counter for Bumper. Smoothing Bumper's ears back with a greasy hand (Bumper was actually a white bunny, though you would never know it by looking at him), he continued his moaning. "I'm afraid we're finished, Bumper. I'm afraid we're done for."

So lost in misery was poor Al that he had completely forgotten Nana.

As for Nana, all of her attention was focused on a small advertisement she found taped to the front of the counter.

A mechanic, thought Nana, *how interesting.*

She looked at poor Al, whose head was dropped so low that his forehead nearly touched the counter.

Well, she thought, *I could certainly give it a go anyway*.

True, Nana did not have any experience fixing cars, but she *had* recently worked as a quality-control inspector in a pencil-sharpener factory—those whizzy sorts with the motors—and how different can one kind of motor be from another?

Of course, Al's wasn't the only predicament on Nana's mind. It did occur to her as well that if she could be of help to Al, perhaps Al might sooner get around to fixing the Dusty Drifter.

And so it seemed, for the time being anyway, that the rodeo would have to wait. What a disappointment this would be to Eufala and Bog—and perhaps you yourself are a bit disappointed, too. A day in a mechanic's shop certainly does not sound nearly as exciting as a day of dust and spurs. Well, rest assured, little buckaroos, this story is far from over. And what's more, things are about to get very interesting.

Nana scooted herself down to where Tuff had been standing and raised her chin to better see Al on the other side. "Excuse me. I'm here about the advertisement for the mechanic position."

"Huh?" said Al, surprised to suddenly see a pair of eyes and a nose directly across the counter from him. Surprised, too, at the mention of the ad. It had been in the paper for three long years, and no one had ever come to inquire about it before. It had become, over the years, something of a sore topic to poor Al. (Like everyone else, you probably didn't even notice the ad in Nana's newspaper this morning. Go ahead and turn back. We'll wait.)

"Oh," said Al. "That."

"I'd like to apply, please," said Nana.

"You'd like to apply?" Al repeated, leaning over the counter to confirm that yes, she was in fact every bit as small and old as he had thought. "Hey, aren't you that bull rider with the broken-down car?"

"Yes," said Nana, "and I should very much like to have it repaired. But, you see, I was thinking—"

"Well, you might as well take it down to Buddy's Garage," interrupted Al, dropping down onto his stool. "Like everybody else."

"But, you see," said Nana, "I was thinking that perhaps if I can help you with that gentleman's car, you might get to mine a bit later on?"

Al looked at Nana and then outside at the cloud of smoke left behind by the Ruffies' cars.

Then at Nana again.

Then at the cloud of smoke.

Finally, he reached into a closet and pulled out a pair of gray overalls. "Here," he said. "See if these fit."

COOKIES
CANDIES
CHIPS
CHIPS
CHIPS
CHIPS
CHIPS
CHIPS
COOKIES
COOKIES
COOKIES

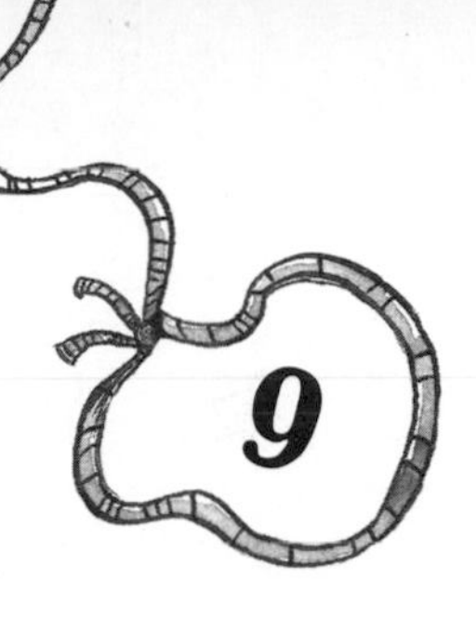

Time to Rustle Up Some Grub

Now the Buy-n-Buy is not called the Buy-n-Buy for nothing. And when you have sixty dollars in your pockets, it might be more aptly named the Buy-n-Buy-n-Buy.

n-Buy.

Especially when you're on your way to your very first rodeo. "RO-DE-O! RO-DE-O!" chanted Eufala and Bog as they flung themselves through the doors of the grocery store.

Inside, they grabbed the biggest cart they could find. After all, there are many things that one might need at a rodeo. You've got your candies to consider, and your chips . . .

"And your more candies," said Bog, grabbing another handful of licorice ropes.

"And your cookies," said Eufala, moving down to the Fudgy Fingers.

"And your more candies," said Bog, digging his hands into a bin of gummy slugs.

"Bog!" snapped Eufala.

Bog looked up with sugar-glazed eyes. "What?"

"Aren't you forgetting a few things?"

"Oh yeah." Bog hurried down to the beverages. "And your sodas."

"And your crackers," said Eufala, tossing a few boxes into the cart.

"And your tape," said Bog, loading three rolls onto his wrist.

"Tape!" said Eufala. "Why would we need tape at a rodeo?"

"In case we want to tape something."

"Oh—," and here Eufala had meant to say "brother," but what came out instead was "hats!"

She pointed at a whole rack of hats up near the checkout.

As everyone knows, you can't go to the rodeo without hats.

"But there isn't one single cowboy hat in here," said Eufala, spinning the rack with such velocity that a half dozen hats flew to the ground.

Bog picked up the brown hat that had landed on top of his shoe. He turned it over in his hands, inspecting it from all sides. Then, without a word, he pulled out a long strand of tape, bit it free with his teeth, and began bending and twisting and taping the brim of the hat.

"There." He held the finished product up for Eufala to see. "A cowboy hat."

"Not bad," said Eufala (which is the most any older sister

can be expected to compliment her younger brother). In truth, though, the hat was quite a bit more than not bad. In fact, if you closed one eye and squinted the other, you might even say it looked just like a real cowboy hat.

Eufala picked out a nice red hat for herself and handed it to Bog, who, with impressive speed and skill, worked his taping magic on it, too.

And now it was time for our two cowpokes to mosey on up to the checkout. But first, a quick scan around the store to make sure they weren't forgetting anything.

If only that woman would get out of their way—that woman who was blocking their view with all her cereal and diapers and—

"Sour cream!" screamed Bog.

Yes, there inside her cart, riding on top of a jumbo bag of diapers, sat one small tub of—

"Sour cream!" screamed Eufala.

"I said it first," said Bog, who, as first to say it, led the way back to the dairy section.

Eufala looked over the various tubs of sour cream. "Who knew torture came in so many shapes and sizes?"

"That Squirty Whip looks good, too," said Bog, whose eyes had wandered a bit too far to the left.

Squirty products! How could they have forgotten their squirty products?

For a while they just stood there, gazing upon that glorious bottle of Squirty Whip. Not only was it "New and Improved," but thanks to

SOUR CREAM
CHIPS
CHIPS
COOKIES
COOKIES

the new active ingredient Mighty Puff ™, it now had 50 percent more squirty action than ever.

It was so hard, so very very hard for them to pick up that tub of sour cream. In fact, should they just get the Squirty Whip and come back for the sour cream later on?

No, they had taken money out of their mother's purse to buy sour cream. And so what did our two responsible children do?

"Come on," said Eufala. She grabbed a tub of sour cream off the shelf as if she were committing the greatest act of bravery. "Let's go."

Park Slugs and Wheely Things

Al led Nana through the little door behind the counter and into the garage where three other mechanics were hard at work. All three had gray hair and gray faces, slumped shoulders, and the same nervous twitch that made their heads jerk back on their necks, as if they suddenly caught sight of a fastball headed their way. (A fairly common condition in Lettuceberg known as Ruffyitis.*)

---

*Other side effects may include skin rashes, stomach pain, occasional light-headedness, night tremors, involuntary whimpering, and a fear of leather.

"That one there is Larry," said Al, pointing to the mechanic working on a black car with skull headlights. "At least I think it's Larry. Larry, that you?"

Larry's head jerked back on his neck. "Yeah," he mumbled. "It's me."

Al looked back and forth between the other two mechanics. "Which one of you is Mick?"

The mechanic polishing the hubcap of a silver car waved his rag in the air.

"So that one over there must be Sue," said Al.

Sue saluted Nana with a windshield wiper.

"How lovely to meet you all!" exclaimed Nana.

The heads of the three mechanics jerked back in unison. Nana took this to mean that they were all pleased to meet her, too.

"And that . . . ," said Al, nodding his head toward a shiny black car, not one dead bug or ding on it anywhere (even the bugs and pebbles knew better than to get too close to Tuff

Blooger's car), " . . . is Tuff's car." And with that, he disappeared back through the little door.

Nana walked up to Tuff's car. "Let's see," she said. "I believe Tuff said something about a park slug."

"Spark plug," murmured the other three mechanics.

"Oh good," said Nana. A spark plug sounded considerably less sticky.

But since Nana hadn't a clue what a spark plug was or where a spark plug was to be found, she thought perhaps it would be best if she observed the other mechanics for a while. She looked around the shop. Larry, Mick, and Sue were all removing one thing or another from the cars they were working on. *Well*, thought Nana, *that certainly is one way to find a spark plug.*

So when Larry removed the headlights from the Ruffy car he was working on, Nana took up her pliers and began removing the headlights from Tuff's car, too.

And when Mick took the doors off another Ruffy car, away went the doors from Tuff's car.

Nana was enjoying herself so much that she began removing more parts from Tuff's car. Then more, and more, and more parts.

The other mechanics were very friendly and seemed quite interested in Nana's work.

"I don't know if I'd be doing that," said Sue.

"Sure Tuff wants you taking his car apart like that?" asked Mick.

But Nana had not yet found anything that looked even vaguely sparky, or the least bit pluggy, and so she continued to remove part . . . after part . . . after part. And when she saw Larry lie down on that little wheely thing and roll himself under a car, Nana thought, *what fun*! And she rolled herself . . . well, she rolled herself . . .

"Oh my," said Nana, returning to her feet. It seemed there wasn't any car left to roll under.

Nana looked down at Tuff's car—or rather, car parts—and felt quite pleased with all she had accomplished. It was, truly, an impressive pile.

But what was it she was to do with this pile of parts?

Oh yes, a spark plug.

And here you may want to pay extra close attention, as something very important is about to happen.

As Nana rummaged through the pile in search of a spark plug, her eye caught on something it had missed before. It was not a metal something or a leather something, not a black something or a gray something. There were no skulls or flames or swords on it anywhere.

In fact, it was shiny. Shiny yellow and red and blue. And it was right down there near the toe of Nana's shoe.

A brochure.

A brochure for—

Nana picked up the flyer and squinted her eyes to better read the twirly writing—*Little Buckaroo Cowboy Camp*.

"Well, that's very interesting, isn't it?" said Nana, and she sat herself back down on the wheely thing for a closer look.

Now, if you remember, Al's Brake Shop was situated at the top of a rather steep hill. But what has not yet been mentioned is that at the back of Al's shop there was a large garage door, and this large garage door was often kept open.

And if you put these two pieces of information together, what you get is this:

Down. (Or, in the case of Butter Street, down, down, down.)

You also get this: Fast.

Nana rolled out the door and shot down that hill like a broken yo-yo—that is to say, like a yo, all down and no up. Past bushes and buses and lawn flamingos she flew. Past the Crispy County Police Department and the Big Top Wig Shop, past barking dogs and beagle scouts, park slides and picnics, not to mention the seven kids on pogo sticks, all of which, by some great stroke of luck, she managed to miss on her way down.

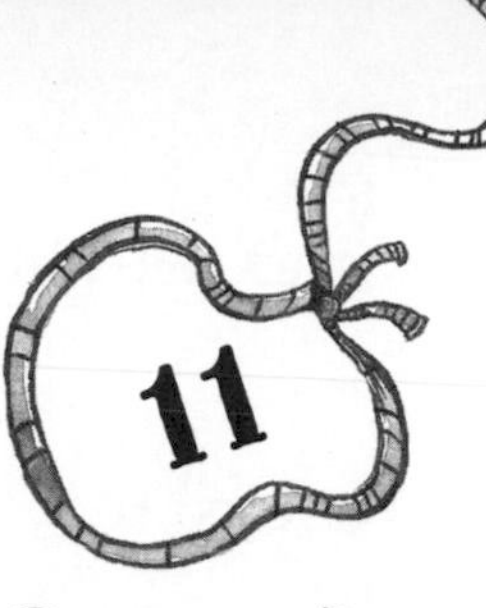

What Goes Down Must Come Up

Nana came to a stop beneath a grape-colored station wagon parked at the end of Vine Street.

"What a drippy one you are," she said up to a pipe that had just leaked a beauty mark down onto her cheek.

Fortunately, Nana found a pair of pliers tucked inside her overalls, and with it she began to tighten the screws and bolts.

"Oh dear, wrong way," said Nana, who now had several moles to accompany her beauty mark, and quickly she twisted the screws and bolts back the other way.

She was nearly finished when a family walked

up to their car to find two shoes poking out from underneath it.

"And there are legs, too," said the little girl.

"Excuse me," said the mother, folding herself over to look beneath the car. "Is there some reason you're under our car?"

"Just one more . . . little . . . turn . . . ," grunted Nana. "And . . . there we go. All done."

"All done?" said the father.

"All done," said Nana. She wheeled out from under the car to find herself no longer inside Al's Brake Shop, but instead in front of the Crispy County Public Pool. "Oh dear, now where on earth am I?"

"You were fixing our car," said the mother, taking a few steps back and pulling her daughter along with her. Fair enough, for it did look as if Nana had contracted a rare form of black chicken pox.

Nana turned to look at the car. "Oh yes, I suppose I was. Well it should run just fine now."

"But it was running fine before," said the father.

"Berny," said the mother, "did you hire someone to fix our car?"

"Mommy, who's that lady?" said the little girl.

"I'm Nana," said Nana, "and who are you?"

"I'm Bibi. I can swim no-handed."

"That's very good," said Nana, wiping her hands off on her overalls. "I would highly recommend a career in oceanography. Though, I must say, the sharks can be a bit of a nuisance."

"Excuse me," said the father, "but we need to go now."

"Oh yes, of course," said Nana. "Well goodbye then! And do come again!" And with the flyer clasped in her hand and the wheely thing tucked like a skateboard beneath her arm, off she headed to . . . oh dear, now where was that mechanic shop again?

Oh yes, *up*.

Sure enough, when Nana looked up, there, between a cloud and a bird, was Al's Brake Shop.

On her way back to Al's, Nana could not stop thinking about that flyer . . . about that happy little cowboy . . . all that red and yellow and blue . . .

She looked up at the clouds above her.

And over to Mr. Bandanna sweeping up outside his shop.

She thought of Tuff.

And of Tuff's car waiting for her back at the shop.

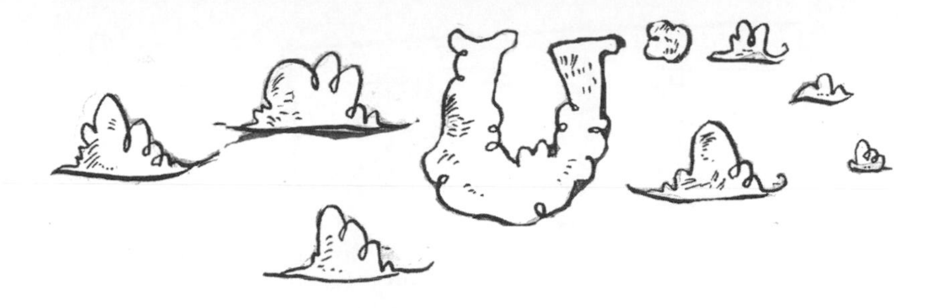

And suddenly it came to her. Suddenly Nana knew what she needed to do to put Tuff's car back together.

Yes, of course, thought Nana. *Of course.*

And this is what she mumbled to herself all the way back up that long hill.

AL'S

Horse Power

Back at the shop, Nana got straight to work. She had very little to do and much time to do it. Or rather, she had much to do and very little time to do it. Yes, that's more like it.

"Now then, I suppose the thing will need a head."

Nana sifted through the pile for something that might serve the purpose. "Ah, there we go," she said, holding up the glove compartment for inspection. "A head."

Now for a neck . . .

A tailpipe ought to do the trick.

"Why are you wearing that suit?"

Nana looked up to find Bog standing behind her.

"I thought we were going to the rodeo," said Eufala, walking up next to her brother.

"Oh yes, the rodeo," said Nana, sifting through the pile for something ear-ish in shape. "Just as soon as I finish this one little project, we'll be on our way. Now let's see, would one of you kindly bring me that wrench over there?"

Though the last thing Eufala and Bog wanted to do just then was fix a car, they figured that if they ever wanted to get to the rodeo, they better pitch in. Besides, they never could resist a good pile of junk—or one of Nana's crazy projects for that matter. And so they dropped their purchases on the ground and joined their grandmother.

Bog managed to locate, retrieve, and deliver a wrench in thirty-seconds flat.

"Here," he panted, handing the wrench to Nana. "I think I beat my personal best."

“Bog,” said Eufala, “finding a wrench isn’t exactly a sport.”

“Thank you, Bog,” said Nana. “Eufala, dear, would you hand me that little tree there? We mustn’t forget to put that back on.”

“But that’s just an air freshener,” said Eufala, handing the little tree to Nana.

“Ponderosa pine,” said Nana, breathing in the fresh scent of cowboy country, “just what we need. Now how about you two help me get that stomach in here.”

“Stomach?” said Bog. “I think that’s the car battery, Nana.”

“Well yes,” said Nana, “but it will have to do.”

And so Eufala and Bog arranged themselves

on either side of the battery and gave it the proper number of grunts to lift it up off the ground and drop it down into the place where Nana's finger was pointing.

"I don't know, Nana," said Eufala once the so-called stomach was in place. "It doesn't look very much like a car."

"A car?" said Nana. "Heavens no. It's not a car that Tuff needs."

Well, you should have seen Eufala and Bog's faces just then. White as cotton balls in a snow-storm. White as the hat they soaked in their mother's bleach. White as the teeth they borrowed from Mrs. Myrtlewood's bedside table. White as . . . well, you get the idea.

What was Nana *thinking* changing Tuff's car into something else? This was not good. This was not good at all. (And leave it to two children who had much experience with disastrous outcomes to know.)

"*Tuff?*" said Eufala.

"But not *the* Tuff. Right, Nana?" said Bog, with a nervous little laugh that made him sound a bit like a squirrel with hiccups.

"Do you know him?" asked Nana, holding a cup holder up to the glove compartment for size.

"He's only the meanest guy in Lettuceberg," said Bog.

"Oh you," said Nana.

"Really, Nana," said Eufala. "We have to get out of here!" She and Bog made a run for the door—only to find, of course, that Nana was still back where they had left her.

"Now let's see then," said Nana, as if she hadn't heard them at all, "just a bit of brown paint—and, oh yes, we could use one of those—what do you call them—one of those mats you put on the floor."

"A floor mat?" said Eufala, moping back toward her grandmother.

"Yes, that's it," said Nana. "Now trot along and see if you can't find us a brown one."

13

Mr. Tasty Toes

Eufala and Bog tried their best to trot, but they just couldn't do it (troubled minds do not make for trotty feet). It was all they could manage just to alternate their legs left and right.

As soon as they were far enough away from Nana, they dropped down behind a Ruffy car for yet another meeting of utmost importance—though in their long history of utmosts, this was perhaps the most utmost of them all.

Their real hope, of course, was that Nana would declare this little fiasco finished, so they could escape before Tuff returned, but as that was highly unlikely, they needed a plan, and they needed one quick.

Eufala sat on a toolbox; Bog cross-legged on a wheely thing.

"He's going to eat her, isn't he?" whispered Bog, the wheely thing rolling him away as he spoke.

"Of course not." Eufala pulled her brother back by his shoe. "He only eats hamsters. And goldfish and stuff."

"He'll eat her toes."

"Maybe," said Eufala, at which Bog let out a series of whimpers.

"Bog," snapped Eufala, "do you want Nana to have feet or not?"

Bog nodded and whimpered some more. This time when he rolled away, Eufala tugged him back by his shirtsleeve.

"Then stop your crying and help me think."

"I'm not crying," said Bog. "I'm whimpering."

"Well, stop your whimpering."

Bog let out one final whine and then searched around his brain for a thought. "How about," he suggested, "we tell him his mom's looking for him? Then when he turns to leave, we bam him on the head with a tire."

"Bog," said Eufala, "Ruffies don't have moms."

"We could tell him his house is on fire," said Bog, rolling away again. "Then when he turns to leave, we bam him on the head with a tire."

"Bog!" Eufala yanked her brother back by his ear. (It was the only thing she could grab in time). "Ruffies don't have houses."

"Ow!" said Bog, rubbing his ear. "His cave then. We'll tell him his cave's on fire," and this time he rolled so far that Eufala had to get up to catch him.

"Bog!" she cried. "Stand up!"

"Why? I'm comfortable."

Eufala lifted one end of the wheely thing, sending Bog tumbling onto his back. "I just thought of a plan."

Perhaps, given an earlier episode in this story, you already know what Eufala had in mind when she carried that wheely thing to the back of the garage. Perhaps you even know what she was thinking when she placed it just inside the opening of the garage door. But just in case:

"As soon as Tuff walks over here," said Eufala, "you push him, and I'll close the door."

"Then 'see ya in Tahiti,' right?" said Bog, happy to have an excuse to use his favorite expression.

"Now all we need is some bait."

"Yeah," said Bog, looking around the garage. "What can we use?"

Eufala gazed around the garage, too, and when her eyes arrived back at Bog—more specifically, at Bog's feet—she smiled.

"Toes."

Bog quickly curled his toes inside his shoes and wedged his shoes beneath a spare tire. "Yeah but, I mean, where are we going to find toes?"

"Not *real* toes," said Eufala, walking around the shop, "fake toes. Toes made out of—" and now she was searching around inside a Ruffy car for something, anything, toe in shape. She opened up the glove compartment, tossed things around, but no toes. Nothing on top of the dashboard or between the seats either.

"Will these work?" said Bog, reaching a hand deep into his pants pocket and digging out five (very fuzzy) gummy slugs.

Well, not only would they work, but those five gummy slugs would turn out to be the very modest beginnings

of what the children would later lovingly refer to as Mr. Tasty Toes.

The rest was a cinch. For two children who had once constructed the Eiffel Tower out of nothing but soap and peanut butter, who had once sculpted the Sphinx of Giza out of panty hose and sliced bread (328 slices, to be exact), finding the makings for a foot was a piece of cake. Well actually, it was five gummy slugs, an oil filter, and some chewed up gum.

Eufala placed the completed Mr. Tasty Toes atop the wheely thing and stood back to admire her work. She felt quite proud of their creation, and she had a right to. Mr. Tasty Toes almost, sort of, if you closed one eye and stood back twenty feet or so, looked just like a real foot.

It was the perfect Tuff trap. As soon as he bent over to take a bite of Mr. Tasty Toes, it was . . .

"See ya in Tahiti!" cried Bog.

"Then we grab Nana and get out of here," said Eufala, starting to walk away.

"So," Bog said nonchalantly (for he assumed from Eufala's frequent hair flips and upturned chin that she had thought of everything), "how are we going to get Tuff to come over here?"

Eufala, it turned out, had not yet considered that important question. She stopped and thought the matter over for a moment.

Across the garage they could see Nana tying the ponderosa pine air freshener around the tailpipe. The vision did not fully register for a good twenty seconds. But on the twenty-first second, Eufala and Bog both cried out together: "Air fresheners!"

By the twenty-fifth second, they were standing before a whole spinning rack of them over by the motor oil and tires.

"Fresh-cut grass?" asked Bog, pointing up high.

"Chocolate mousse?" said Eufala, pointing down low.

And then, at the exact same moment, their eyes landed on the perfect air freshener. Right there in the center of the rack. "Roasted hot dog!"

Grabbing a handful each, they began laying them out along the floor, beginning at the little door at the front of the garage and leading all the way up to, you guessed it, Mr. Tasty Toes atop the wheely thing.

And then, with a slightly improved trot, the children headed back to Nana.

"Here you go," said Eufala, handing Nana the brown floor mat they had borrowed from one of the Ruffy cars.

"Very good," said Nana. In return, she handed the children each a paintbrush and set them to work painting what she matter-of-factly referred to as the legs of the car.

Eufala and Bog did their best. Well, perhaps not their *very* best. Generally it is a good idea to look at the object one is painting, but Eufala and Bog were finding it very difficult to do so. Twice already they had painted each other, and once Bog even painted his own shirtsleeve because they simply couldn't keep their eyes from wandering over to that little door.

But eventually, yes eventually, they did manage to relax, and before long were busily painting away.

While they lathered up the legs with brown paint and Nana saw about attaching a hubcap to the battery, Bog entertained the group with his impersonations, first of Officer Burly:

"My mama used to give me Fudge Freezies whenever I got owies."

Then of his teacher Mr. Fleagal:

"Please explain to me, Mr. Bog, what an earwig catapult has to do with classic literature."

And next his impersonation of Tuff:

"What do you mean it's not done?"

"Oh my," said Nana, setting the hubcap down to give Bog a much-deserved round of applause. "Now that was very good, Bog."

And it was, too.

There was just one tiny problem:

It wasn't Bog.

Get Your Fresh Toes!

As Nana continued working, the children dropped their brushes and made for the door that led to the front desk. (Larry, Mick, and Sue, on the other hand, dropped their tools and made for the back door that led to *saving their necks*.)

The office door stood open just enough for Eufala and Bog to see Al standing—or rather slouching—or rather slumping—behind the counter.

"What part of me turning you into a bumper sticker don't you understand?" Tuff yelled. Seven Ruffies stood behind him, all with sneers and crossed arms.

"Sure, okay, Tuff," said Al. "Say, have you had a chance to check out our new line of mufflers? We have Loud, Extra Loud, Extra Extra Loud—"

"Why's he talking about mufflers?" whispered Bog.

"It's called stalling," whispered Eufala. "You'll learn it in third grade."

"Stop your stalling," said Tuff, "I want my car NOW."

And NOW is exactly when Tuff and that pack of Ruffies started for the door.

There was no time to think . . . they had to . . .

"Excuse me, Mr. Tuff," said Eufala, bursting through the door before Tuff could burst through the other way, "but—"

"But what?" said Tuff.

"But—," said Bog, peeking out from behind his sister.

"WHAT?" growled Tuff.

"But—" squeaked Eufala.

"WHAT!" gruffed Tuff.

"Would you care for some toes?" peeped Eufala.

"Yeah," said Bog, "do you want some nice, delicious toes?"

"Why would I want toes?" barked Tuff.

"Because they're really fresh?" said Eufala.

"Just the way you like them?" said Bog.

"Yeah," said Eufala, "can't you *smell* them?"

Unfortunately, they may as well have been tossing tulips at Tuff for all the good their words were doing. With every sentence they sputtered, Tuff and his gang of Ruffies took one step closer. It was a bit like that game Red Light Green Light, only without the red lights. They just kept coming and coming and . . .

"Ouch!" said Bog, who had walked straight back into the jaggedy ear of Nana's creation.

Fortunately, thanks to countless escapades involving windowsills, barbed wire fences, and tree limbs, the children were quite bendy and

managed to arrange themselves in a way that might (at least they hoped) block Tuff's view of his—well, for now, let's just call it a car.

"Hello, dear!" Nana called when she saw Tuff and the Ruffies walking her way.

Tuff, who figured Nana must be talking to someone else, stopped and turned to look behind him.

Each of the seven Ruffies beside him turned to look back, too, for not one of them could imagine someone thinking him a dear.

"Nana," whispered Eufala, "maybe you shouldn't show him his car right now."

"Yeah," whispered Bog, "maybe you should wait."

"Now wait one minute," said Tuff, who unfortunately had the keen hearing of a bat. "What are you two trying to pull?" He narrowed his eyes until they were practically closed. "Why don't you want me to see my car?"

"Because it's not ready?" said Eufala.

"Oh they're just being silly," said Nana, turning around to look at what appeared to be a cheerleading formation behind her.

"You mean it's done?" said Tuff, his eyes opening a fraction—1/32 of an inch to be precise. "My car's done?"

"Of course it is," said Nana.

"Why didn't you say so in the first place?" and with that, Tuff pushed past Nana, then Al, then Bog and Eufala until he came to:

15
Not Exactly a Yee-Haw

A long moment of silence followed. And in that long silence, Tuff's face changed from pink to fuchsia to scarlet to a very lovely shade of maroon—at least Nana thought so.

"I need to go to the bathroom," whispered Bog.

"Nice try," whispered Eufala. Just to be on the safe side, though, she dropped him down from her shoulders. "If we leave," she hissed to the heap of Bog down on the floor rubbing his elbow, "who will save Nana from Tuff?"

Bog looked around the room for something in the way of a superhero—even a gangster or thug would do—but all he came up with was a trembling Al. Eufala was right; it was up to them. And with brave and noble thoughts swelling in him, with his spine a little straighter and his neck once again visible between his head and his shoulders, he took his place next to Eufala.

And back they went to that awful silence, except now Al's face was changing, from shiny to sweaty to downright drippy. Every time he looked at one of the Ruffies, with their twitchy jaws and their necks like tree trunks, a new bead of sweat rolled off his chin and dropped to the floor.

Only Nana seemed comfortable. She simply stood there, a pleased look on her face, not a care in the world, as the silence went on, and on . . . and on . . .

And On...

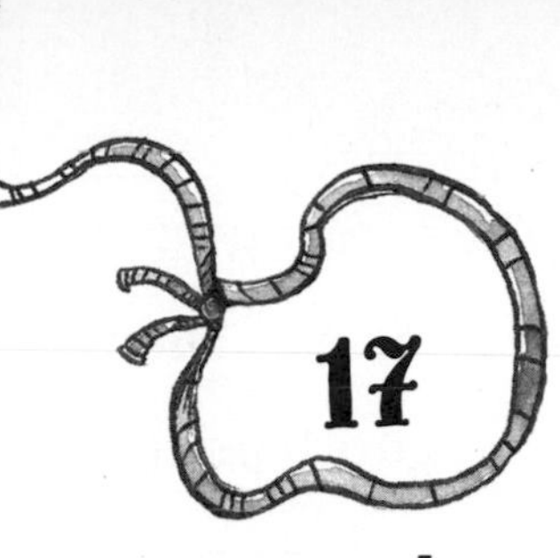

17

SuperBog to the Rescue

All that can be said about what happened next is that it was pure brilliance. It was sheer inspiration. And it came from none other than our very own Bog.

Yes, Bog, with his two years less experience than Eufala in tactics of distraction and trickery, Bog, who so seldom managed to get his words to come out right, said the one perfect thing. "Um, excuse me," he said. "Mr. Tuff?"

Actually, that wasn't the one perfect thing. It was what he said next:

"Cool horse."

At once, Eufala recognized the genius of Bog's words. And, as his mentor, she did not hesitate to take a good portion of the credit. "Yeah," she said. "Cool horse, Mr. Tuff."

And that's when it began to happen. That's when the genius began to kick in.

First one Ruffy, then two, and within seconds a whole pack of Ruffies had crowded around to admire Tuff's horse.

"Hey, that's pretty alright," said one.

"Yeah, I've been thinking about doing something like that to my car," said another.

And on down the line it went.

It was certainly clear how the Ruffies felt about Tuff's horse. But just how Tuff felt about Tuff's horse? That remained to be seen.

And what's worse, he was walking straight for Nana.

Return of Harry

Tuff stopped two inches in front of Nana (and Eufala and Bog, who had placed themselves in front of Nana), and for a moment he just stood there. With the strangest expression on his face . . . as if his lips could not decide what to do. Nor his eyes. Nor his nose for that matter. (It was an awful lot of scrunching for one face.)

Then Tuff did something he hadn't done since he was a very little boy.

Tuff Blooger hugged somebody.

He reached out his cornstalk arms, wrapped them around Nana—and Eufala and Bog, who were still in front of her—and lifted them right off the ground.

And he squeezed, and he squeezed, and he—oh dear, this was not good—it seemed as if he might squeeze the air right out of them. And Bog, who was underneath Eufala, who was underneath Nana, was getting the very worst of it.

Fortunately, just as Bog had begun to contemplate his short life on Earth—what he might have done differently, who would cry the hardest when they heard the news, who would take all of his toys—and what about his candy!—*oh, for the love of God, not his candy!*—Tuff gently lowered the trio back to the ground.

And when he set them down and released his arms, Tuff was not the same old Tuff anymore. Tuff was—well—let's just say that Tuff Blooger has blue eyes.

He even has sparkly blue eyes.

Especially when he smiles, which he just did. Right before he skipped off—yes you heard correctly, Tuff *skipped off*—to join his friends.

And to pat his new horse, of course.

"There now, Liberty," he said, as he stroked the glove compartment.

"Hu . . . hu . . . hu," said Bog, still recovering from Tuff's hug.

But before he could say "How did you know Tuff wanted a horse?" Eufala said, "How did you know Tuff wanted a horse?"

"Well, it seemed to me," said Nana, "that there was only one part missing from that car, and it wasn't some silly old spark plug."

"Which part?" asked Bog, looking and sounding a bit more three-dimensional.

"Tuff."

"Oh," said Bog, even though it would take approximately 27 more hours for him to fully understand what Nana had meant.

“And you two weren’t such bad mechanics either.” Nana placed an arm around each of her grandchildren, and the three of them stood there watching what had fast become a very enthusiastic round of show-and-tell. One Ruffy had pulled a stuffed monkey from his pocket; another, a model rocket. There was a book of poetry and a train whistle, a mandolin and a butterfly net. One Ruffy had laced on his tap shoes to demonstrate his shuffle-step.

And the strangest sight of all? They were all—all eight of them—smiling.

And where was Al during this party of sorts?

Well, it was a show-and-tell after all. And so Al had gone back for his own little secret possession—who was only too happy to be freed from his long captivity beneath the counter.

LETTUCEBERG
COUNTY
RODEO

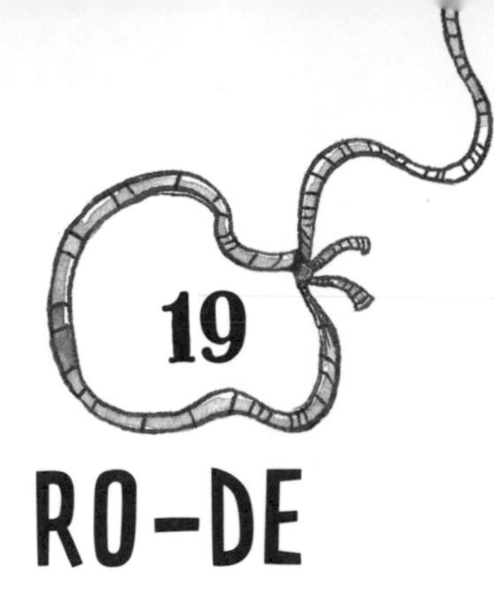

RO-DE

“O!” said Bog.

Yes, they were finally on their way to the Lettuceberg County Rodeo.

No, not in Nana’s car. The Dusty Drifter would require a bit of work, unfortunately—as well as several parts ordered from another century. But that’s okay. Harry (as he now prefers to be called) graciously offered to provide the transportation.

When they got to the fairgrounds the rodeo was in full swing, which, for a rodeo, means enveloped in an enormous cloud of dust. There was bronco busting and barrel racing, steer roping and cow-chip tossing, and, compliments of Eufala and Bog, the first ever cotton-candy eating contest.

Nana stood in line with Harry, practicing her lassoing in preparation for the big steer-roping competition, while nearby Eufala and Bog befriended a bull named Sally and just beyond them, Elaine made her way across the bullring—

Elaine?!

Oh no! How did she ever find them?! She must have used her maternal instinct (of which she possessed approximately 18 times that of most mothers). That or she had already checked everywhere else in town (she did look a bit haggard).

Bog spotted her first.

"Here's your sour cream," he said, wincing and holding out the tub as if it were a shield that might protect him from his mother's wrath. If you are not familiar with the word *wrath*, it is often accompanied by a screechy voice and wildly waving arms.

"Do you know you two have been gone for *three* hours? Anything could have happened. You could have been . . . you could have . . . you —" but before she could go on to list the many tragedies that might have befallen her children, something even more distressing caught her eye:

Nana.

No, it was not that alone. It was what Nana was doing. She was swinging a lasso in the air and hollering something that sounded a bit like *yee* followed by what sounded something like *haw*.

But it was not just that either. It was *who* Nana was *with*. Holding her arm as she swung the rope round and round was—

Tuff?

"What on earth!" exclaimed Elaine, waggling her way across the rodeo grounds (waggling, *n.* a motion that occurs when one is in a hurry and yet very concerned about getting cow dung on one's shoes).

"Oh hello, dear," said Nana when she spotted her daughter walking toward her—and at an impressive clip, too.

Elaine grabbed her mother by the shoulders (ruining a perfectly good wind-up throw) and hissed in her ear "Do you have any idea who that *is*?"

"Why, yes. This is Mr. Harry Blooger," said Nana. "Harry, I'd like you to meet my daughter, Elaine."

"Pleasure to make your acquaintance, ma'am," said Harry.

"Mother," said Elaine, her teeth clamped tightly together, "may I have a word with you?" She took Nana by the arm and guided her toward the bleachers. But, of course, just as she began to sit her mother down, her eyes fell upon one of them there, too. A Ruffy, right there in the bleachers.

In fact, no matter which direction Elaine turned, there seemed to be another one. They were everywhere—playing horseshoes, eating hot dogs, square dancing, entering their pies in the pie contest . . .

And do you know what one of those Ruffies did next? He walked right up to Nana—with Elaine standing right there—and said, "Excuse me. I was wondering if you could fix my car, too."

"Well," said Elaine, absolutely aghast, "you obviously have the wrong person. My mother is old and—"

"Hey," interrupted the Ruffy, leaning in for a closer look at the butterfly pin fastened to Elaine's blouse. "I like that pin you're wearing."

Well, you can imagine Elaine's surprise.

"I said I like that pin you got on," the Ruffy said again, for Elaine was still too shocked—and more than a little flattered—to speak.

"My . . . my pin?" she said. "You like my pin?" Elaine almost never blushed, so what you are about to witness is a very rare sight indeed. "Oh," she said, the pink in her cheeks spreading to her ears, "it's just a little something I found."

"*Lerodea Eufala*. It's one of my favorites, too," said the Ruffy, rolling up his shirtsleeve to reveal a lovely *Lerodea Eufala* right there on his forearm.

What children? Tuff who? For the rest of the afternoon, Elaine forgot all about her worries. She was, for one brief period of time anyway, a carefree woman.

As for Eufala and Bog, they were only too happy to be forgotten by their mother. While their mother talked butterflies with Roger (formerly "The Razor"), and while Nana tried her hand (or you might say, her derriere) at bull riding, Eufala and Bog were off enjoying their very first taste of a real live rodeo.

And boy did it beat ranch dressing.